Mr. Russell

A
TOURNAMENT
OF KNIGHTS

written and illustrated by
Joe Lasker

Thomas Y. Crowell
New York

To Rebecca Rose

A Tournament of Knights
Copyright 1986 by Joe Lasker
Printed in the U.S.A. All rights reserved.
1   2   3   4   5   6   7   8   9   10
First Edition

Library of Congress Cataloging in Publication Data
Lasker, Joe.
    A tournament of knights.

    Summary: Justin, a young knight in the Middle Ages,
prepares to engage in his first tournament, while an
experienced challenger plans to defeat him.
    [1. Tournament—Fiction.   2. Knights and knight-
hood—Fiction]   I. Title.
PZ7.L3272To 1986   [E]   85-48075
ISBN 0-690-04541-7
ISBN 0-690-04542-5 (lib. bdg.)

A Note to the Reader

When I was a child I read many stories about knights, but when I worked on this book I learned interesting things I hadn't known before. For instance, I didn't know that when knights fought, the loser became the victor's prisoner and had to pay him a ransom to be set free. Usually this ransom was the loser's horse, arms, and armor. I used to wonder why a knight would fight to the death. Now I see that it was because he could lose not only his honor, but his most precious and useful possessions.

When knights were not fighting in a war, they played at war—in a "tournament." To the people of medieval times, the violent tournament was an important entertainment, as a big-league sports event is today. Tourneys took place six hundred years ago, when everything was different. Times have changed, but some of today's entertainment is still violent. When I look at today's prizefighter or quarterback I think of Rolf, the knight-errant in this story.

J.L.

Baron Orlando sent forth his heralds. They rode from kingdom to kingdom, proclaiming, "A tournament! Come ye to the tournament in honor of Lord Justin, who has been made a knight! Come, good people, to my lord Orlando's castle for the tournament!"

Peddlers, beggars, pickpockets, and dancing bears mingled with the festive crowds that came to the tournament. The visitors arrived and set up their tents in the peaceful fields and hamlets surrounding Baron Orlando's castle. They would live in the tents until the tourney was over.

From the highest tower of the castle, Lord Orlando and his son Justin looked silently down at the crowd and tents.

My son will bring us great honor, thought the father. This grand tournament will bring fame to the name of our family.

I could bring us dishonor if I lose a contest, thought Justin. This grand tournament then would ruin our good name. As he scanned the landscape, he thought, My father owns all this. His wealth will attract a knight-errant who is hungry for land. If he should defeat me, he would demand half my father's barony as my ransom.

"You will prove yourself worthy," said Baron Orlando.

"Perhaps," whispered Justin, "perhaps."

The tournament would cost Baron Orlando much money, and each knight who took part would find the tourney expensive, too. He had to own horses and sets of armor, weapons, and shields. He needed tents, banners, wagons, and other supplies, as well as several squires—noble-born young men who served a knight in return for training in knighthood.

One of the knights drawn to the tournament was Sir Rolf. Seeing the immense castle and merry crowds, he sighed. There had been no costly tournament when he had become a knight many years ago. His father, a poor nobleman without land, could not afford to shower him with gifts. All he could give his son was advice: "Be a knight-errant and fight for profit. Fight for honor and chivalry *after* you have wealth and power."

Rolf had no choice but to heed his father's advice and follow the tourneys. A giant of a man and a courageous fighter, he learned to slash and batter his way toward riches—risking, winning, and losing fortunes. And from the knights he defeated he sought more than the usual prizes of their horses and armor: Sir Rolf also demanded land and peasants.

Rolf and Justin were among the knights and noble gentry who assembled in the castle the day before the games. They had all come to review the knights' weapons and banners. Heralds checked the coat-of-arms and history of each contestant. Only knights of noble birth ("true knights") could fight in a tourney. The judges of the tourney inspected each weapon, making sure that edges and points were blunted. Then the knights pledged to obey the tournament rules.

Following these ceremonies everyone sat down to a lavish banquet. During the meal, Sir Rolf sought out Justin. "I want a closer look at you," he said, "for we shall meet in combat."

"And what do you see?" asked Justin.

"I see you have the movement and lightness of youth," said the older knight.

"By your age and scars I see that you have the advantage of experience," Justin replied.

Sir Rolf smiled. "Then we are fairly matched."

Justin shook his head. "I think not. I know your reputation, and I would rather break bread with you than cross spears."

Rolf gently placed his huge hand on Justin's shoulder. "Alas! We must fight because you are the richest prize here. That is how I live. I have no choice."

"I have no choice either," replied Justin. "Honor forces me to accept your challenge."

Well before sunrise on the first day of the tourney, the heralds broke the sleepy silence. "Let the jousters make ready!" they cried up and down the avenues of tents.

The squires were already awake and starting their chores. Each had to feed and brush his master's horse; polish and grease the armor for the knight and his steed; dress the horse in its harness, armor, long cloths, and saddle; and lay out the knight's cushioned undergarments, which he would wear under the hard, uncomfortable armor. Finally, the squire laid out the many pieces of his master's suit of armor.

Then the "squire of the body," without whose help no knight could put on armor, assembled the suit on his master. The knight stood patiently for two hours as the squire adjusted and tightened rivets, hooks, hinges, laces, buckles, bolts, spring pins, straps, and clasps.

The burning sun was high in the sky as spectators, eager to get good places, left the cool shade of their tents. They hurried to the "lists," a fenced area in a large, open field. Here, in the first action of the tournament, the knights would divide into two teams and fight a mock battle, or "melee." In the second part, the same knights would take turns jousting: two mounted knights, armed with lances, would race toward each other on opposite sides of a fence, or "barrier." The losers in any of these games would become the victors' prisoners and had to pay them ransom.

At last everything was ready. Lord Orlando rose from his seat in the royal lodge, bowed to the noble guests and judges, and declared, "Let this grand tournament in honor of Lord Justin's knighting begin!"

Trumpets and drums sounded as a procession entered the lists. First came the heralds, blowing horns. Then came the squires, leading the warriors—sixty "true" and splendid knights, their armor flashing in the sun. The cavalcade paraded around the lists to lusty applause and shouts: "Bring honor to your noble families! Think upon your ladies!"

As the knights passed the lodges, the noble ladies waved and blushed. The cavaliers showed off, puffing out their chests and holding their heads higher. The women knew the fine points of jousting. They threw souvenirs to their favorite

heroes. Justin caught a glove that was tossed to him and gallantly attached it to his helmet, as was the custom. Soon colorful handkerchiefs, ribbons, belts, sleeves—even strips of cloth torn from skirts—fluttered from the helmets and lances of the horsemen.

The presence of ladies was an important part of the tournament. Every knight, according to the code of chivalry, had to have a lady to fight for. If he had no lady, he secretly chose one. She did not need to be aware of this honor; she could be a stranger. A chivalrous knight was ready to die, if need be, to protect his mistress from danger or insult. He asked nothing in return. It was reward enough if she looked sweetly at him or permitted him to wear her handkerchief or glove on his helmet as a symbol of her admiration.

The first event of the tourney, the melee, began. The contestants divided into two teams, facing each other, with the chief herald between them. Justin, not wanting to fight Rolf, looked about warily for the knight-errant. With relief he saw that for now, at least, he did not have to worry. The heralds, his father's subjects, had placed them both on the same team. The heralds were like referees;

they kept tally of victories, defeats, and fouls, and observed everything closely. The chief herald raised his sword and shouted, "In the king's name, do your battle!"

With lances pointed straight ahead, the knights on the two opposing teams charged, colliding with the shock of a thunderclap. Lances splintered and

shattered, hurling dangerous chunks of wood and metal toward the spectators. Through the fray, Justin could see a few knights go down while the rest fought close in with swords, axes, maces, flails, and war hammers. This was the melee—a mock but brutal battle. The valiant nobles showed off their combat skills, cracking skulls and breaking arms. (But they were careful never to strike a horse, for they would be disqualified.)

At great risk, squires ran into the bloody tumble, bringing fresh weapons and

rescuing those fallen masters who, unable to get up under the weight of their heavy armor, were being trampled under the horses' hooves. Soon Justin and the others were covered with the thick, choking dust from the sun-baked field. Steel clanged against steel as sweating cavaliers tried to impress the ladies and judges with their skills. Wounded knights were carried out, others limped away, disgraced at having been unhorsed, and the spectators shouted for more. The violence raged for fully one hour before the judges ordered a halt.

When the melee ended, Justin waved to his father, who shared his joy at having passed his first test in combat.

"Lords, ladies, knights and squires, noble hearts, and gentle souls: come to the castle this evening." Baron Orlando summoned his guests to a splendid feast, but not all the knights could attend. Some rested in their tents, suffering terribly from deep wounds. A few knights lay across anvils while blacksmiths worked to free them from their crumpled armor.

The banging of hammers awoke Justin early the next morning. Carpenters were building the long jousting barrier down the middle of the lists for the second part of the tourney, the three days of jousting.

"Bring on the jousts!" commanded Lord Orlando, opening the day's games. Trumpets sounded, and the chief heralds called out, "Let Lord Oscar and Lord Percival come forward!" Squires led the two horsemen to opposite ends of the barrier. The jousters closed their visors to signal that they were ready. The chief herald raised his sword and shouted, "For honor and glory, charge!"

The crowd cheered as the husky war steeds thundered forward. The cavaliers pointed their lances at each other and bent low behind their shields, bracing for the shock. CRACK! The barrier prevented a collision, but the recoil was strong enough to throw both horses back on their haunches amid a shower of turf and splintered lances.

"Well struck! A brave course!" shouted the spectators. Though dazed by their lance-shattering impact, both men remained in their saddles. Neither had won. They wheeled and returned to their stations, ready to continue. Their squires ran to them with fresh lances and shields.

Justin watched from the sidelines. When would Rolf's challenge come?

Another course, another clash, and more shattered lances. Each worthy missed his opponent in the third course, but in the fourth running, spears broke. This was the third spear breaking, so the rules dictated that the evenly matched warriors dismount and fight on foot. Oscar drew his sword, Percival his ax. They swung furiously—slashing, smashing, crumpling shields and armor. Blood trickled from the steel suits. The sun beat down, sapping their strength. Finally Lord Oscar sagged to his knees and toppled over.

More jousts were run before the heralds and trumpets called an intermission. Cakes and ale were served in the lodges. The baron's marshals tossed loaves of dark bread to the commoners and beggars.

When silvery trumpet notes signaled the end of intermission, the people rushed back to their places. But before the names of the next two jousters could be announced, a huge knight galloped boldly into the lists. "Lord Justin, come forth!" bellowed Lord Rolf. "I challenge you to a duel!"

Justin hesitated. A hush fell on the assembly, and all eyes turned to him. He reached for his lance and shield and spurred his charger into the lists.

Justin and Rolf reached their stations at opposite ends of the barrier and closed their visors to signal their readiness. Through the eye slits in his helmet Justin looked at the hulking challenger, whose polished armor sparkled in the hot sun. Justin heard the muffled sound of trumpets and saw the chief herald's sword rise and fall. Digging in his spurs, he felt the thumping of his heart and the pounding hooves of his horse. From inside his hot, dark helmet, he saw Rolf looming larger and larger. Justin gritted his teeth, leaned forward, and aimed his lance at the center of Rolf's shield. The foes crashed with a sudden dizzying impact.

When he was able to focus his eyes again, Justin saw that his lance had been shattered and that Sir Rolf had failed to unseat him. He wheeled and cantered back to his station, passing Rolf, who also held a broken lance. The spectators were on their feet, waving and shouting, "Nobly done! Fairly broken!"

The sun beat down on the suits of armor, heating them until they were as hot as ovens. Justin, younger and lighter, was better able to withstand the heat than Rolf. Sweat poured into Rolf's eyes, his vision blurred, his arms grew heavy in spite of his great strength.

Armed with new lances and shields, Justin and Rolf charged again. This time Justin's lance smashed squarely into Rolf's shield, pitching Rolf from his saddle with such force that he went rolling and clattering in the powdery dust.

The spectators cheered thunderously, but Justin was too shaken to respond. As Rolf's squires ran to help their master to his feet, Rolf looked up at Justin and said, "It would have been better to break bread than to cross spears."

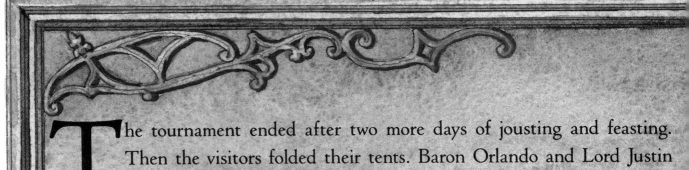

The tournament ended after two more days of jousting and feasting. Then the visitors folded their tents. Baron Orlando and Lord Justin watched from the castle's highest tower as the last guests departed.

"You fought bravely," said Orlando.

"Sir Rolf was the better man," said Justin. "It was his bad luck and the sun that felled him. I was stiff with fear."

"But you kept going," said his father. "That took courage. I'm proud of you." Then he put his arm around his son.

Glossary

Baron One who owned land and ruled people and was loyal to no one but the king.

Barony The area a baron ruled.

Charger A knight's horse.

Chivalry The medieval knight's code of ideal behavior. A chivalrous knight was brave and honorable, protected the weak, and treated his enemies generously.

Coat of arms A picture on a shield or banner that identified a noble family name.

Gentry People of noble rank.

Herald A tournament official who regulated the events, made announcements, kept score, and was a specialist in coats of arms and family histories.

Joust A duel on horseback between two knights carrying lances.

Knight A mounted, armed nobleman wearing armor.

Knight-errant A knight with little or no property who rode from tournament to tournament trying to gain property by winning ransoms from defeated opponents.

Lance A knight's weapon with a very long wooden shaft and a steel head.

Lists The fenced-off ground where knights fought each other in a tournament.

Melee (pronounced may-lay) A free-for-all fight between two groups of mounted knights.

Ransom A payment that frees one from captivity.

Rules of the tournament A set of laws regulating the conduct of the contestants. Tournaments had no standard rules: each lordly sponsor made up his own.

Squire A nobly born youth who, at about age 13, began years of training for knighthood by serving a knight.

Steed A horse.

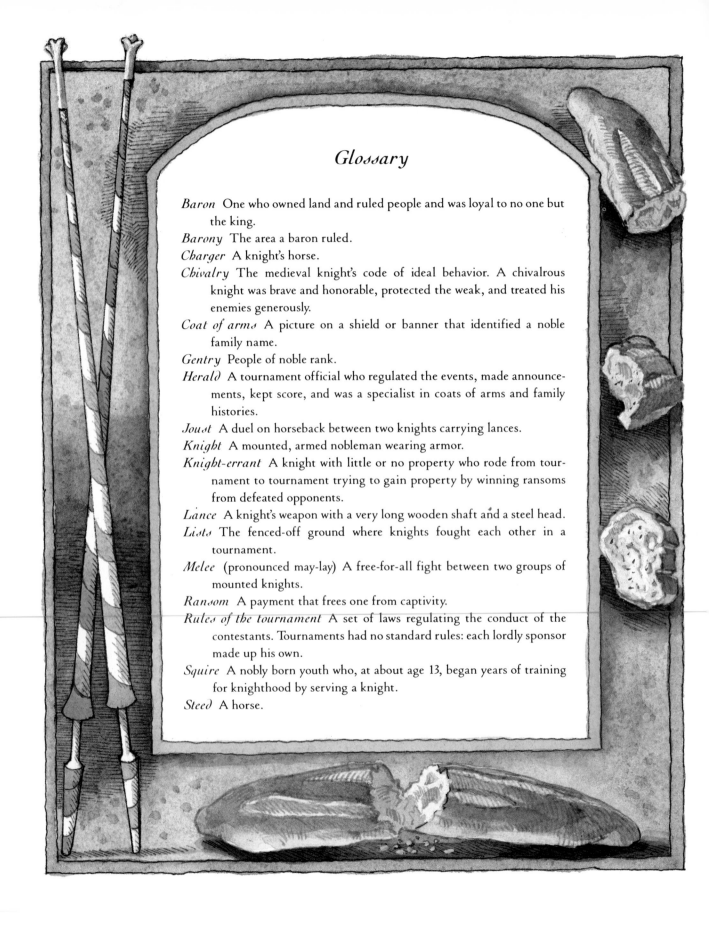